Ra
Me

by Paul Stewart
Illustrated by Bill Ledger

Houghton Mifflin Harcourt.

In this story ...

Nisha
(Nimbus)

Nisha has the power to control the weather. She can make it sunny or stormy. Once she stopped some baddies by trapping them in a tornado.

Jin
(Swoop)

Ann
(Boost)

Mrs. Molten
(teacher)

The **Sophos Comet** is a vast ball of ice and space rock that whizzes around the solar system. Unlike other comets, it is thought to be made from powerful, super-charged rocks.

Every five years, the Sophos Comet flies past Earth causing a **meteor shower** (where space rocks called meteors make streaks of light in the night sky). Anyone born during this meteor shower has the gift of superpowers.

Occasionally, during a meteor shower, a chunk of the meteor lands on Earth and becomes a meteorite. **Sophos Meteorites** are special because the super-charged rock can boost superheroes' powers. Some people even believe they can *give* you superpowers.

Chapter 1:
The Meteor Shower

Ray Ranter was standing on a balcony at Ranter Tower, staring up at the night sky. A bunny-wunny was at his side.

"If only I had superpowers like those pesky heroes," Ranter said. "I could take over Lexis City once and for all."

Just then, a ball of yellow light hurtled across the sky.

Ranter gasped. "A meteor! Maybe it's from the Sophos Comet. If so, the meteorite will give me the superpowers I need!"

"Th-nn-th-th," the bunny-wunny snuffled.

"You're right," Ranter replied. "I must find it ... and fast."

Meanwhile, at Hero Academy, the superheroes saw the meteor streak down from the sky too....

Look! It's heading for Wildcroft Woods!

Do you really think it can boost our superpowers—or even give people powers?

We'd better find the meteorite before any villains do, just in case!

In another part of Lexis City, Boulderman was on the roof of Rock House. He also watched the meteor pass overhead.

"I'm going to find that meteorite," he growled. "And when it has boosted my powers, I'll destroy Hero Academy once and for all!"

Many years ago, Boulderman had been a student at Hero Academy. Unfortunately, Boulderboy—as he was called back then—was often in trouble.

School report

Real name:
Frank Stone

Superhero name:
Boulderboy

Superpower:
can make rocks appear in his hands

End of term report:
Frank is a gifted student, but he must learn to control his temper. This year, he smashed Mrs. Molten's lab, the cafeteria, and five classroom windows.

Signed: The Head

Boulderboy felt that the Head was being unfair and left Hero Academy, never to return.

Chapter 2:
A Walk in the Woods

"Quick! Everyone off," Mrs. Molten said, as she parked the school bus at the edge of Wildcroft Woods.

Nisha jumped off the bus, shivering in the early morning air. She spun into her superhero costume and became Nimbus. Beside her, Jin and Ann were soon dressed as Swoop and Boost.

Mrs. Molten rummaged in the storage locker of the bus for the gadgets she'd brought to help find the meteorite. "Here, take this heat locator," she said to Swoop. "Boost, I have a metal detector for you. Last but not least...." She handed Nimbus an extraterrestrial tracker to detect space material.

Just before they set off, Nimbus noticed two cars in the parking lot. "Do you think they belong to villains?" she asked.

"If they do, they've already got a head start," Boost replied.

"We don't have a moment to lose," Mrs. Molten said, urgently. "That meteorite must not fall into the wrong hands."

As they went into the woods, the sound of birds singing filled the air. Then, suddenly, they heard something else.

Bleep. *BLEEP.* **BLEEP**....

"My metal detector," said Boost excitedly.

Moments later, Swoop's heat locator started to buzz. Then Nimbus's extraterrestrial tracker let out a shrill whistle. Soon, the woods echoed with a bleeping, buzzing, whistling din.

"The meteorite must be somewhere over there!" said Nimbus. As she pointed, a zigzag bolt of lightning shot out from her fingertips. Nimbus cried out with surprise. "My whole body's tingling," she said.

"So is mine," replied Swoop.

"*And* mine," said Boost. She leaned against a tree to rest for a moment ... and pushed it over. "Wow!" she exclaimed. "I'm stronger than ever."

"It's the Sophos Meteorite," said Mrs. Molten. "As we get closer, it's supercharging your powers." She frowned. "It must be nearby. I wonder why we can't see it?"

"I'll take a look," said Swoop. He jumped off the ground, then soared up into the air so fast that the others lost sight of him in seconds. Moments later, he was back beside them.

"I didn't see the meteorite," he said breathlessly, "but that was a-*ma*-zing! I flew so fast and so high, I almost went into orbit!"

"You must all be careful, and try to control your supercharged powers," Mrs. Molten warned them. "Otherwise, who knows what might happen?"

Just then, Nimbus sneezed. Hailstones the size of tennis balls came hammering down from the sky.

"Sorry," she muttered, as she stopped the hail shower.

Chapter 3:
Deeper Into the Woods

"Let's move on," Mrs. Molten said. "Quickly now, and keep a sharp lookout. If there *are* any villains around, they might have set traps."

Mrs. Molten strode ahead, with Nimbus close behind her. Swoop followed next, and Boost was at the back. They all walked as fast as they could through the dense undergrowth, while keeping an eye out for anything suspicious.

"We *must* be getting near the meteorite by now,"
Boost shouted above the bleep-bleep of her
metal detector. "I ... AAARGH!"

She had stepped on a net that was hidden
beneath some leaves. The net had shot up into the
air with Boost inside. Now she was trapped!

Boost looked miserable. Swoop flew up and hovered next to her.

"I'll get you out of there soon," he said. Then he called down to Mrs. Molten and Nimbus. "You go on. We'll catch up."

Mrs. Molten frowned. "I'm not sure about leaving you."

"This proves there are villains around. You have to find that meteorite before they do!" Boost cried. "Every second counts."

"Boost is right," Nimbus said. "We should keep going."

Mrs. Molten sighed. "All right. Be careful!"

She and Nimbus walked on through the woods, but it wasn't long before they ran into problems of their own.

"That's strange," Mrs. Molten said. "It seems to be getting foggy."

"It's not me this time," Nimbus replied.

"Could you make it go away?" Mrs. Molten asked.

"I'll try," said Nimbus. She summoned a breeze, but the fog wouldn't clear. "It's not like normal fog."

They stumbled. They tripped. They cried out.

"I can't see a thing!" Nimbus exclaimed.
"Mrs. Molten, where *are* you?"

"Over here!" came the reply, but Mrs. Molten's voice was faint.

They were getting separated from each other.

"Mrs. Molten?" called Nimbus. "Mrs. Molten!"

There was no reply. Nimbus was on her own.

Telling herself to be brave, Nimbus kept going.
Then she heard a low hum up ahead.

Property of
Ray Ranter

Nimbus followed the noise and—*THUNK!*—bumped into a large, metal box.

Attached to the box was a long funnel, with fog pouring out of it. Nimbus spotted a nameplate on the side of the box: Property of Ray Ranter.

"I might have known," Nimbus muttered. "I can guess why Ranter is using a fog machine—he's after the meteorite." She turned off the machine, and the air slowly cleared. "Now I need to find that villain, and fast!"

Chapter 4:
The Clearing

Nimbus took a deep breath. With the others gone, it was up to her to find the meteorite.

Just then, Nimbus spotted some footprints. She followed them until she could see a clearing up ahead. Then she heard the sound of raised voices. She hid behind a tree and peered around it.

There was the meteorite! It was half-buried in the earth. The ground around it was steaming.

There were also two people in the clearing. One of them was Ray Ranter, but Nimbus didn't recognize the other one. Tall and powerfully built, he looked as though he was made of rock. He and Ranter were arguing.

"I see you managed to avoid my traps," Ranter snarled. "No matter. I'll deal with you now, Boulderman."

"You'll never defeat me!" Boulderman bellowed.
"You don't even have any superpowers."

"Soon I will. This meteorite will give them to me,"
Ranter told him.

Boulderman roared with laughter. "No it won't!
You only get powers if you're born during a Sophos
Comet meteor shower."

"That's what you think!" Ranter fumed.

"The meteorite is mine!" Boulderman shouted.
"I'm going to become bigger and badder than ever.
Then I'll destroy Hero Academy!"

"If anyone's going to destroy Hero Academy," Ranter yelled back, "it'll be *me*."

Nimbus shuddered. Destroy Hero Academy? She had to stop Boulderman *and* Ranter at all costs.

"Stay away from that meteorite," Ranter warned.

"Or what?" Boulderman demanded.

"Or this!" cried Ranter.

Nimbus gasped. Suddenly, a bunch of bunny-wunnies emerged from the trees. They started to pelt Boulderman with carrots.

Boulderman stumbled back. He clapped his huge hands together and an e-*nor*-mous rock appeared.

Boulderman was about to throw it at Ranter when the bunny-wunnies leaped up and tickled him. Boulderman shrieked with laughter and dropped the rock. It fell to the ground, sending a shower of dirt all over Ranter.

"My beautiful white suit!" Ranter cried out. He glared at Boulderman. "Nobody messes up my suit. You'll regret that!"

As the battle continued, Nimbus turned her attention to the meteorite. It still looked too hot to handle and much too heavy to move.

Nimbus raised her hands and concentrated hard. Seconds later, it began to pour with rain. It wasn't just any old rain, though. With her super-charged powers, Nimbus created rain that was so hard and so heavy, it poured down like a waterfall.

Steam rose from the meteorite as it cooled. The clearing where Ranter and Boulderman were still fighting started to turn into mud.

As the ground became a muddy swamp, the two villains sank up to their ankles. They didn't seem to notice, though. They were too focused on stopping each other from getting to the meteorite.

Still hidden behind the tree, Nimbus waited. When Ranter and Boulderman were knee-deep in the thick mud, she put the second part of her plan into action. Nimbus stopped the rain and turned the air ice-cold.

"I can't move!" Boulderman yelled, as the mud froze solid.

"Neither can I!" Ranter whined.

"Now for the meteorite," Nimbus said to herself. She closed her eyes and concentrated, until she could hear a rush of wind. Then she opened her eyes and smiled. She had created a whirlwind! Nimbus pointed it at the meteorite. The whirlwind moved toward it and, with a loud *POP*, plucked the meteorite from the earth.

The meteorite hovered in the center of the whirlwind, and Nimbus steered it out of the clearing and into the trees.

Stuck in the frozen mud, Ray Ranter and Boulderman could only stare as the meteorite swirled away.

As Nimbus and the whirlwind headed into the woods, she heard the two villains arguing.

"This is your fault!" Boulderman roared.

"No, it's your fault!" Ranter snarled back.

"Your fault!"

"*Your* fault!"

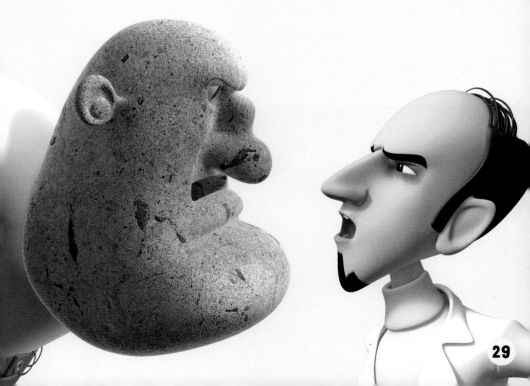

Keeping the spinning whirlwind under control, Nimbus made her way back through the trees. When she reached the parking lot, she saw the others standing next to the school bus.

"I've been so worried!" Mrs. Molten exclaimed. "We tried to find you, but it was hopeless in all that fog. I ended up walking in circles. I just got back!"

Nimbus lowered her hands. The whirlwind stopped spinning and the meteorite dropped lightly to the ground.

"You got it!" Swoop said.

"Nice work, Nimbus!" Boost said, smiling.

"Now, let's get it safely back to school," added Mrs. Molten.

Chapter 5:
Back at Hero Academy

The Head congratulated Nimbus on finding the meteorite. "All the best meteorites have a special name," he said. "Nimbus, as you found it, you shall have the honor of naming it."

"How about the Sophos Supercharger?" Nimbus suggested.

The Head agreed that it was the perfect name. "The meteorite is so powerful that I'm going to lock it away safely," he said. "It won't be able to supercharge your powers from inside my reinforced vault, but no one will be able to steal it either."

At least, that's what everyone hoped....